GOOD NIGHT, OLIVER WIZARD

Rebecca Kai Dotlich

ILLUSTRATED BY Josée Masse

BOYDS MILLS PRESS

AN IMPRINT OF HIGHLIGHTS

Honesdale, Pennsylvania

It was time for all wizards to go to bed.
And so it was bedtime for Oliver Wizard.

He put on his moon pajamas, his star slippers, and his magic cape. He scooted his small stool to the window.

Oliver pointed his wand and named the stars: "I see wishing stars and spell stars and stars *just being stars*."

"Wizards know lots of things," said Daddy.

The wind whistled and the window rattled. Oliver shivered and waved his wand while saying his best and most magical spell: *"Light or dark, dark or light, stay away scary things tonight."*

"That should do it," said Daddy.

Oliver pointed his wand. "There shall be cereal!"
Daddy played *Follow the Wizard* to the kitchen.
"But then," he said and pointed to the clock, "there shall
be sleep." Oliver nodded.

Daddy played *Follow the Wizard* back upstairs. "Sparkle!"

Oliver swirled his cape and clicked his teeth. "Like stars?"

"Like stars," said Daddy.

Oliver stopped in the doorway. "I think it's too dark."

"Say your best and most magical spell," said Daddy.

Oliver waved his wand. *"Light or dark, dark or light, stay away scary things tonight."*

"That should do it," said Daddy.

Oliver waved his toothbrush.
"Look at those stars!" said Daddy.
Oliver giggled. He swirled his cape.
"Are wizards brave?" he asked.
Daddy rubbed his chin. "Sometimes yes
and sometimes no."
"Like me," said Oliver.
"Like you," said Daddy.

Daddy pointed to the bed.

Oliver pointed to the bookshelf where *The Big Book of Wishing Stars* was right where it always was.

Daddy plopped into his big chair. "See," he said, as he opened the book, "you're full of magic."

Oliver touched his wand to daddy's nose.
Daddy sneezed.
Oliver giggled.
Oliver waved his wand back and forth. "Poof!
We are *invisible*!"
Daddy nodded and pointed to the clock.
"Even invisible wizards need sleep."

"What's the magic word?" asked Oliver.
"Scat," said Daddy.
Oliver giggled. "Not that one!"
"Wobbletywink," said Daddy, and he scooped
up Oliver and whisked him off to bed.

Oliver stared at the window. "I might imagine wild things."

"Whisper your best chant," said Daddy.

"I might see scary shadows," said Oliver.

"Wave them away," said Daddy.

Oliver waved his wand *whoosh* to the ceiling and
whoosh to the floor. "Like that?"
"Like that," said Daddy.

"I might hear a deep croak from the dark corner," said Oliver.

"Tell the toad to go to sleep," said Daddy.

Oliver giggled. "I won't even need my wand for that."

"One more spell?" asked Oliver.
"Just one," said Daddy.
"There shall be *pancakes for breakfast!*"
"And there shall be sleep for wizards," said Daddy.

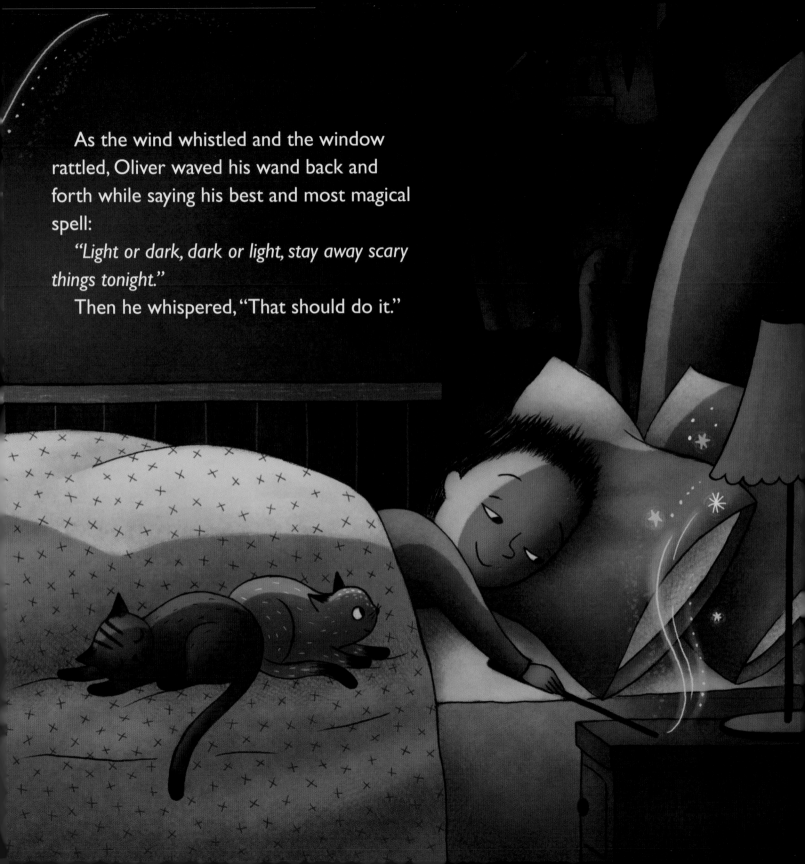

As the wind whistled and the window rattled, Oliver waved his wand back and forth while saying his best and most magical spell:

"*Light or dark, dark or light, stay away scary things tonight.*"

Then he whispered, "That should do it."

Good night,
Oliver Wizard.

To a real wizard of an editor, Rebecca M. Davis,
for loving Oliver for so long.
And to all those who name and wish on stars.
—RKD

For Luc and Alice, with all my love —JM

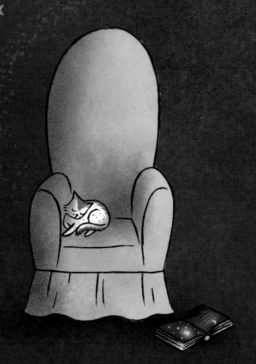

Text copyright © 2019 by Rebecca Kai Dotlich
Illustrations copyright © 2019 by Josée Masse
All rights reserved. Copying or digitizing this book for storage,
display, or distribution in any other medium is strictly prohibited.
For information about permission to reproduce selections from
this book, contact permissions@highlights.com.

Boyds Mills Press
An Imprint of Highlights
815 Church Street
Honesdale, Pennsylvania 18431
boydsmillspress.com
Printed in China

ISBN: 978-1-62979-337-5
Library of Congress Control Number: 2018962344
First edition
10 9 8 7 6 5 4 3 2 1

Design by Barbara Grzeslo
The text is set in Gill Sans.
The illustrations are done in mixed media—a combination of
drawings and digital.